EPISODE ONE

It rained heavily like never before as if the cloud could no longer hold the water together and out of anger released the water on the earth. It rained heavily for hours and not just that, there was this thunderstorm and everyone got scared. No one could go outside so everyone had to stay indoors all through.

Sweet! Sweet! I wonder where she went too, could she probably be somewhere else, Maggie spoke out loudly. Sweet, poor girl had gotten tired responding to everyone's request, has she had to attend to everyone all by herself. She was happy in the morning doing her chores, the day was bright and clear she had wet the plants that morning and even fed the animals all alone.

She could have asked for help but she felt she could do it alone, not quite long, the weather changed with wind coming from the forests. The wind probably connived with the cloud that day as it blew off trees, plants and roofs away. She ran as fast as her legs could carry her into the house. She had to attend to everyone in the house has no one could go out because of the rain.

Sweet, Maggie tapped her on her shoulders has she woke up speedily. Ma'am how may I help you my lady? I need you to make coffee for me and yes I want it quickly. Yes ma'am as she walked quickly to the kitchen. Maggie knew how tired sweet must have been. At a point she felt sorry for the little girl who had been with her since she was six years old.

Mother! I don't want to get married, I am scared. Maggie you are not a kid anymore, you are eighteen already and also I can't do anything because it was your father's decision not mine. Yours is even better I got married at the age of sixteen, you have to support your family Maggie and the only way to do that is to get married to the Heir of Mercity, Ned.

I really know you don't want too but please you have too, so that this family won't be put to shame only you can take away this reproach away from us. Maggie cleaned the tears running down from her mother's cheek and assured her not to worry anymore, I will get married to Ned. As Maggie walked out of the room Natasha felt bad for her only daughter but there was nothing she could do about it. It was for her own good too.

Steve walked in with a little girl dressed up in dirty linen, she looked so unkempt and famished. Honey, who is she? And want is she doing in our home? Get me some water to drink woman! As he walked towards the chair and sat. The little girl looked around and for the first time saw a house bigger than hers.

The house was painted with white, it was really beautiful to behold, she saw portraits hanged on the wall. Some expensive artworks done by rich and famous artists, she wasn't happy that she had to leave her own family, but somehow she felt this peace within and knew she will be treated with love and care.

Maggie gave the water to her dad as she looked at the little beautiful maiden standing in front of her. She didn't know why she felt attached to her, she walked towards her and asked her for her name, the girl kept quiet and couldn't talk. She looked at Maggie with fear in her eyes, I don't know if you once had a name but I will call you sweet from now henceforth that because you are beautiful.

Ann smiled, she had a name but was shy to respond, but she sure loved the name Sweet and Maggie too. Steve and Natasha was happy that both of them were getting along pretty well. They had always wanted to have more children but end up having just one. They knew how much their daughter had always longed for a playmate.

Maggie please show her to her room, so that she can freshen up, not to worry dad I have got this. She held her hands as they both climbed the stairs. Honey, now that Maggie isn't here, can you now tell me where you get the little lad from? Her dad brought her to the office today and handed her over to me since he could not pay back his debts. How unfortunate, poor little girl, Natasha felt pity for her but was happy that her daughter won't be alone anymore.

The reason why I brought the girl over, is because I want her to keep Maggie company when she leaves here to her husband's house. I want her to have someone of her own, someone she can trust. You know how dangerous the family of Mercity is, I don't want her to be alone and helpless there. That is a good idea, she walked over to where Steve was and pecked him on his cheeks. I will make dinner now so that we can all eat.

Ma'am, here is the coffee I made your favorite. Are you okay ma? You look so tired. Sweet, I just want to thank you for having my back all these years, it has been twenty years now and you are still this sweet girl I met when you were just six. Thank you sweet, she walked out f the room.

Sweet wondered what must have happened for Maggie to reach that way. She has really come to love Maggie and her family, Maggie had always been nice to her. She just hoped everything was okay with her as she pondered on.

EPISODE TWO

Ned to Dan let's go to Mercity in full it is known as merchant village, it was an empire built by Ned's father when he was a young adult. Liam Dan's grand father has always loved horses while he was a little kid and has always dreamt of having a stable, but he wanted something more, an empire of his own. Something that would generate money and lasts for generation to come. So he worked hard for years, serving other people until he was able to save up and start his own empire. He sells the best horses and is known not only in Kunash but also in other neighboring cities.

Before Liam's death he had transferred everything he had to Ned and Ned was planning on doing so too. Dan was happy as he walked with his father, his father workers were also delighted to see him as they knew, he would soon be their boss. Dan left his father, who was talking to their oldest employee as he walked around the place. He loved horses just like his granddad. There was this horse that caught his attention, a black horse with blue eyes. Dan went closer to the horse and strolled it's hair, he felt like the horse wanted to tell him something but he couldn't understand . Buddy I don't know what your trying to say to me but I will sure figure it out. He tapped the horse back softly and walked away.

Blackie what are you trying to do? Spokie asked. Can't you see, I was trying to inform him about the danger ahead, if he only he could hear me. Poor lad Blackie said as he walked further away. Blackie where are you going to? Spokie followed. We are horses and they are humans, it will be hard for them to understand or even hear us. That true though I just wish there was a way to go about it. Don't worry Blackie everything will be fine, I hope so too.

Dan where have you been, I have searched everywhere for you. I am so sorry dad I just went to see the horses in the stable. It's alright son have a seat. So you see son my father left this empire for me to take care of and I have been running this empire for the past two decades it will be your turn soon. I want you to prepare your self ahead, you need to be strong my son. It won't be easy but I want you to know that you can.

You are no longer a kid anymore, you are now a young adult, gradually becoming a man. You are an heir, you shouldn't see yourself as less. You have servants, make good use of them to your advantage. If you must succeed then you must learn not to trust just anyone you must be determined, be consistent in whatever you do. My son, be wise, do not jump into hasty conclusions. Take your time, remember time reveals all things. There is nothing hidden under the sun.

I have heard you father and I will do as you have said, thank you dad. You can leave now, I have something to take care off, take care dad, he walked out of the office and shut the door behind him.

I wonder what is at the other side, as he looked towards the forest, he had never left Kunash city before, his parents had always told him this was were he belong too, he was still curious to know. He had heard from people in the market that there was another city far away, and that after one must have crossed the forest and a stream.

Asher had been searching everywhere for Dan his friend, though he was a servant working for Dan's family but however they both managed to build a strong friendship that even Dan's parent couldn't separate them. We heard from the servants that Dan went to Mercity with his dad, and had asked sweet to prepare his favorite snacks so he could take to Dan. He had gotten to the empire and he hasn't seen Dan, he checked the stable first because he knew how much he loved horses but he wasn't there, he wondered where Dan was.

As he walked closer to the field he saw Dan sitting on the floor, Dan what are you doing here sitting in this manner? Oh! Asher, my dear friend I was just curious to know what was at the other side. Oh! You brought my favorite didn't you? Asher handed over the snacks to him as he ate it up hurriedly.

One day if ever you decide to go to the other side, please take me along with you Dan. Sure why not, give me your hands. Asher stretched out his hands, and before he knew it be found himself on the floor with Dan as they both laughed.

EPISODE THREE

No!!! Ned screamed as he woke up and realized that it was all a dream. Maggie rushed to her husband's room, honey, I heard you scream hope your fine? She looked so worried as she shifted the curtains to adjust them.

The sight of lightning made her more scared, I am okay dear, it was all a dream. Please can you get me a glass of water to drink, sure will be right back. Here is your water, she stood besides his bed. I can't tell Maggie about my dream, no I can't.

Maggie knew there was something bothering her husband, he is definitely hiding something from me, she couldn't help it but didn't want to bother him, so she left him alone all to himself.

It showered a bit but Ned went out despite the dark clouds. I need to visit the fortune-teller, but he has to disguise himself so as not to create attention. He went with Asher, he didn't know why he preferred Asher among his other servants, he felt Asher could be trusted and he wasn't wrong anyways.

Asher led the horses through the secret passage that only he and his master knew off, as they rode their horses out of the compound, Asher wondered where they were heading to but he couldn't ask his boss even if he wanted to.

Ned got to the place and entered into the house which looked deserted and scary, it was though no one had lived in the house for years, he saw cobwebs lingering around the door and corners, he even saw candles arranged in an unusual manner. He went further into the house as he left Asher at the gate. Asher just hoped that his boss comes out safely, he didn't know he reason why they were here but the just hoped they leave anytime soon.

Sweet can you check who is at the door, yes ma'am. She opened the door and who did she see, Jim Ned's best friend. There was this aura he had and she didn't like it at all. Come on in, she said, he thanked her and went straight to the living room to sit. Oh! Look who we have here, it has been a while you last visited, I thought we won't be seeing you any time soon. So sorry Maggie I have been busy with work lately. It's okay, thank God you are here now. You look as beautiful as ever Maggie, thank you Jim has she sit on the couch opposite him. What would you like to take? Anything is fine but a glass of juice will do.

Sweet get Jim a glass of juice. Jim you are almost fifty and you haven't gotten married yet, I am just being concerned about you. You know you are my husband's best friend and like a family to us. Sweet hands over the glass of juice to him and walks away. Well Maggie, I would have loved to get married and have a family of my own but since the day, the girl I loved got married to someone else I couldn't help but remain single.

Oh! Dear, I am so sorry I didn't mean to bring up the past, you must have been hurt badly, so sorry once again dear. It's fine Maggie that was a long time ago, besides it all in the past now. Where is Ned? Ned he stepped out, he should be on his way now. Will you wait for him? No dear so sorry I can't, probably I will come and see him some other time, thank you for the juice. I should take my leave now, okay dear, take care and please be fine, she shut the door behind him.

I just hope he is happy with his decisions, it must have been hard for him to stay alone all these years. I wonder where Ned went to, she looked out through the window, it might rain soon. Sweet have you seen Asher today? I have been searching everywhere for him, young master he went out with your dad, your dad will be back anytime soon. Thanks sweet, what are we having for dinner? I am famished, we will be having fried potatoes and tomato sauce. Sweet set the table, my husband is home, so that we can all have dinner together.

EPISODE FOUR

I have waited years for this day to come and finally my plans are coming into reality. Well Maggie enjoy it while it lasts because your going to be mine soon. He took his glass of wine and laughed out all to himself. Ned you think you can get away from me, you took everything from me and even the woman I loved because you were richer than I was. I am going to get back at you and no one will be able to deliver you from my hands.

Asher could not believe what his boss just told him, he knew Dan was his own friend but him asking this kind of request, he knew something was wrong but he still couldn't ask his master. Ned to Asher, please take good care of my son, don't leave him alone, support him and counsel him like a brother would.

I know you are both fond of each other, I wouldn't be able to pay you for doing this but I if I could I would. No sir, you don't have to pay me for taking care of Dan, he is my friend and also like a brother to me.

I will do all that I can to support and protect him I promise. Ned felt he could trust Asher but he couldn't tell him what the fortune- teller told him, that he had to keep to himself. He had something he wanted to give to Dan on his forthcoming birthday.

Singing and humming has she walked happily greeting everyone she met on her way to the market. There was no more vegetables at home , and she needed to get things ready, today is Dan's birthday. She couldn't believe it herself, she was there when Maggie gave birth to him. The day of his birth was a unique one has their was an eclipse that day, she has heard stories while she was little that anyone given birth to on the day if an eclipse has a great destiny and also will face lots of trials in life, she just hope the boy will be happy forever.

She was lost in deep thought that she didn't know when someone dragged her bag from her. The thief ran fast that she couldn't catch up with him, she screamed for help and all of a sudden, Carl came from no where and ran after the thief. He knew the corners of the market and their hideouts so it was easy for him to catch the thief. He collected the bag of money from the thief after beating the hell out of him. He saw sweet and handed over the bag of money to her, here this is yours, thank you sir.

What is your name she asked? My name is Carl, what yours? My name is sweet. Such a lovely name for a beauty like you. She blushed hard and it was obvious as her cheeks turned red, that was the first time she was hearing such. He noticed and smiled to himself. Carl was a very handsome young man with blonde hair and green eyes. He had a very nice physique and looked masculine, he was very good looking to behold, every girls dream.

Are you here? Carl had been talking the whole time but unknown to him sweet wasn't even listening has she was lost in thoughts. Sorry, come again, thanks Carl I am grateful I have to be on my way now. Nice meeting you Carl, thanks for your help. She walked away into the market, she turned back after walking some few meters, she wanted to take a good look at the gentleman once again. She just felt like it was all a fairytale, she had heard stories about snow white and Cinderella she Wondered if this was how they felt when they met their prince charming.

Carl wondered if the girl was okay, maybe she is still shocked over the whole incident that just happened, poor girl she must have been frightened. He jumped on his horse and rode off towards the border of the city. He has been sent on an errand by his master, he didn't want to get on his master's nerve. He kept on pondering about the whole event that happened few minutes ago as he rode faster towards the border.

EPISODE FIVE

Blackie what are you doing here all alone? Why are you not joining the rest at the stable? I don't feel like, besides I love my own company Spokie. I know you do Blackie but you still need the rest horses, you can't live alone, we are all you have got Blackie. What are you doing here Spokie? Well, I didn't see you around so I decided to come check here for you, besides you're my friend. Smiled, I didn't know I was your friend, you always acted like you didn't like me when we were together with the other horses.

You even joined them in teasing me. I am so sorry about that Blackie, I didn't know you to be this kind, caring and fun to be with until lately. You see Spokie you don't get to know how others are until you get close to them. You don't judge one at a distance, or base your conclusions on what you have heard from others concerning that person. You come closer and get to know the person for yourself and can now judge based on your observations and the time you have spent with that person Spokie. I used to think you were proud and rude. Me, proud and rude, why do you say so? Well I and the others knew that you were everyone's favorite here in Mercity, you enjoyed all the attention and we all got jealous of you. I am so sorry Blackie , it's fine Spokie we are cool now, really?

Hey!! Lower your voice, I can hear some voices, lower your voice, okay Blackie as they both walked towards the direction of the voices. So what is the plan? I heard Ned will be traveling next month and why is that? Well he didn't disclose the reason to us during the meeting, but I heard from the oldest worker that it was for a business. It could be he wants to meet with his business partners. Okay your doing a great job, hands over the bag of money to him. I will get back to you soon remember this is only between us.

Spokie did you see that, that is a conspiracy against Ned. What are we going to do? Blackie you just have to wait, besides even if we want to expose them no one will hear us or even comprehend what we say have you forgotten that we are animals and they are humans. Don't do anything stupid yet, besides from their conversation they will be having more meetings, we just have to follow them up so that we can know how to help Ned and his family.

Thanks Spokie, that is very nice idea, but that face looks familiar, I know I have seen that face somewhere I can't just remember where. Thank you for your help, anything for you Blackie as they both walked back to the stable together.

Happy birthday son, I love you so very much my dear child. Hope your enjoying your day, birthday party? Yes mum I am, thank you so very much mum. I love you too as he hugged her and pecked her cheeks. Here, take this, I got this for you as your birthday present. I hope you like it dear, opens the parcel and saw a beautiful Necklace. It's an Emerald necklace wow! It's sparkling mom. Thank you mum I love it so very much he hugged her once more this time more tightly. He wore it on quickly, it suits you well my son. Thanks mum has he walked away from her room happily to greet his quests.

Dear nanny Lindy, I don't know where you are presently, but I do miss you, thank you for this wonderful present that you gave to my son Dan. Nanny Lindy was the one who took care of Dan when he was born, her mother sent her over since she couldn't come over. She knew

Maggie has to experience or knowledge whatsoever in taking care of a

new born baby. Nanny Lindy took care of Dan as if he were her own

biological son, she stayed with them for five years and returned back to

her mother even after Maggie begged her not to return. She refused and

said she had to go back to her mother even after Maggie pleaded with

her not too.

Before, she left, she left this Emerald necklace with Maggie and

asked her to give it to Dan on his twenty-two birthday, she didn't know

why she kept that present all this years but was glad that she did fulfill

nanny Lindy last wish.

How time flies, she walked out of her room, she didn't know why

she felt the way she did. She had this mixed feeling, she was happy

today is her son's birthday and also she was sad for no reason. If only

she understood that, that was a sign maybe she could have been able to

avert the danger coming her way.

Welcome Jim, it's been ages now as they both hugged each other

and laughed. Please get my friend a bottle of wine and some fried chickens, have a sit, thank you my friend, has he sat on the single chair his eyes met Maggie's . She didn't understand why his presence is making her feel uncomfortable, but he is still her husband's best friend and she had to greet him.

Hi! Hello Maggie, hope your enjoying you're the party Jim? Sure yes I am, you look beautiful, he took good look at the woman standing at his front, she hasn't changed one bit, just the same way he saw her years ago, she blew his mind away and even today she still did. Your dress looks so nice on you, he looked at her in a seductive manner. Thank you Jim, you don't look bad either, she walked away from his presence to get a glass of water for herself, that man sure makes her feel uncomfortable.

You can't run away from me anymore Maggie, you will be mine soon, I will have you all to myself at last. Here you go pal, he hands over the glass of wine to him. I heard from Maggie that you came over to the house the other day. I came around Ned but you weren't around and Maggie seems not to know where you went to. I had something urgent to take care of, okay buddy, where is the birthday boy? I have got something for him too. Dan!! Uncle Jim is here to see you.

Here comes the birthday boy, here you go, has he hands over the gift to him, your growing into a handsome man. I am sure your father is proud of you. Thank you uncle Jim, he left the two man to enjoy their company.

At the kitchen, sweet was happy, she always has so many people to attend to. She was getting worn out but she was happy nevertheless it was Dan's birthday, she remembered when Dan was a little boy and how stubborn he was, he won't even listen to anyone not even his parents except it was from nanny Lindy. She missed her too.

Please can I get a glass of water? Sweet knew she had heard that voice some where before, she turned and saw Carl, surprised what are you doing here? His he one of Dan's friend? If he was one definitely she would have seen him around. Too may questions kept coming.

Carl knew what she was thinking and decided to feed her with the right answers, because he knew assumptions could be deadly. I am here for the birthday party, I came with my master. Can I have the water now, yes sure here you go, she was about asking who is master was? But before she turned to ask he was no where to be found.

EPISODE SIX

Two months later, Dan was worried. It has been over a month that his

had travelled on a business trip and has not returned. It was unlike him,

he just hope everything is okay with him? Maggie knew something was

definitely wrong with her husband but she was helpless. There is nothing

she can do but to hope that her husband comes back from his trip soon.

Poor Dan, I just hope he is fine, I wish I could help him but how are

you going to help him? Even if you want too, I don't know yet Spokie as

he walked farther away from her. Ned isn't going to return, on his way

he was ambushed and killed. Are you sure of what your saying Blackie?

Yes sir, the assassin confirmed his death, that great news I have to

inform my boss immediately.

Your really doing a great job as he ends the call. Soon we shall take

over Mercity and everything therein.

Spokie, Dan is in great danger, I have to save him. How are you going to do that? I have to come up with something quickly, we have no time.

Where have you been sweet? I have been waiting, sorry Carl I had to attend to Maggie, you know she has been totally down since her husband travelled and has not returned. I feel for her seriously she doesn't deserve all of these. What of Dan? How is he coping? Dan is trying to be strong for himself and Maggie. It hasn't been easy for him too, especially managing the affairs at Mercity. I heard he is even having issues managing the workers who feel he is way to young to be their boss.

So sorry sweet for everything that has happened, you know I love you right? I really do, I will do everything I can to make you happy has he held her closer to himself.

Carl was feeling so sorry, he never wanted to play with sweet emotions, but he has a wicked boss who had threatened to kill his family if he refused his orders. Jim had found out about him and sweet and has made him used her aa a bait. He just have to act as though, he was in love with her and manipulate her in order to gain information of what going on in Ned's house. He felt sorry ,but there was nothing he could do too, he was helpless.

Dan looked at the script in his hands and wondered what Could have happened to his dad. After his birthday party, his father had called him and gave him the script, in it is information that will help you, make you happy, rich and even sustain your family in the future, it will reveal mysteries to you and be a guide in this journey of life. You must not open the script until your twenty-five, if you do you shall face the consequences attached to it. Scared and happy at the same time, he collected the script and thanked his dad.

Was his father aware that he was not going to return, he wanted his father to come back, he is still having issues handling the affairs at Mercity and there is mum who is now a shadow of herself. He hid the script has he heard a knock on the door, come in the door is opened.

Asher walked in looking sad, master I am sorry to inform you but we have to leave now!

It's too dangerous for you now, what do you mean leave this place? I heard an information that some people have been sent to kill you. What! Okay what about mum? I am sorry we will have to leave her here. What nonsense are you saying? I can't leave mum all to herself here, I just can't. Come on Dan we don't have time, we need to save you first, you can come for your mother anytime.

You have to trust me Dan, we have no much time left. Asher opened his wardrobe and picked as many clothes as he could, before they knew it Dan saw some men clothed in black rushing into their house. Let go Asher, they are here, he took the script along and left with Asher. Where are we going to pass? The front door is filled with men already, don't worry follow me there is a secret passage that I and your dad knew about.

Blackie was part of the horse Asher took. They both jumped on the

horses and rode off, but unfortunately one of the men saw them from

Dan's window and chased after them.

Sweet ran upstairs to Maggie's room to inform her about the whole

situation. Maggie came downstairs and saw the men, what do you want

from us? Leave my family alone, she walked up to a man and pushed

him. Woman stay out of this in anger he slapped her and she fell on the

floor. Sweet rushed to her rescue, leave my son alone has she cried

helplessly.

You can cry all you want, but your son will end up just the way your

husband did, he laughed out wickedly and walked away. Maggie could

not believe her ears, so her husband is dead, someone killed him, she

screamed the more and cried helplessly, she just hope nothing bad

happens to her only son. Please save my son she cried out.

The man pursued after them and kept shooting arrows at them as they

ran into the thick forests. Blackie ran faster, as fast has it legs could carry him, he had always wanted to protect Dan. More men kept running after them, Asher knew he had to do something in order to save Dan's life.

He stopped and asked Dan to continue, Dan didn't want too, but Asher told him that was the only way he could save him. Dan continued the journey as Blackie ran faster, he felt bad leaving Asher all by himself, he didn't know why all these was happening and why? He just know he needs to be alive, Asher had sacrifice his life just I save him, he need to live at least.

Asher fought off the men but one kept chasing after Dan, he shot an arrow, and the arrow fell Dan's bag on the floor where he had is script, he couldn't stop, he needed to save his life first, so he kept running. Blackie took a different route and the man lost them. Dan escaped with Blackie but missed his friend and script. He travelled for three days with Blackie until he got to another city. He was happy that he was alive but sad. He looked at Blackie and said seems like we got only ourselves now

buddy, as he fell on the grass.

The
script
Merit Nwobugwu